I Wish I Were an Alien

School Specialty
Publishing

Text Copyright © Evans Brothers Ltd. 2004. Illustration Copyright © Lisa
Williams 2004. First published by Evans Brothers Limited, 2A Portman Mansions,
Chiltern Street, London W1U 6NR , United Kingdom. This edition published
under license from Zero to Ten Limited. All rights reserved. Printed in Hong
Kong. This edition published in 2005 by Gingham Dog Press, an imprint of
School Specialty Publishing, a member of the School Specialty Family.

Library of Congress-in-Publication Data is on file with the publisher.

Send all inquires to:
8720 Orion Place
Columbus, OH 43240-2111

ISBN 0-7696-4020-6

4 5 6 7 8 9 10 EVN 10 09 08

I Wish I Were an Alien

By Vivian French

Illustrated by Lisa Williams

GINGHAM DOG PRESS

Columbus, Ohio

I wish I were an alien.
I would float around in space.

I would not have to clean my teeth.

I would fly around the planets.

I would zoom around the stars.

I would go and check out Jupiter.

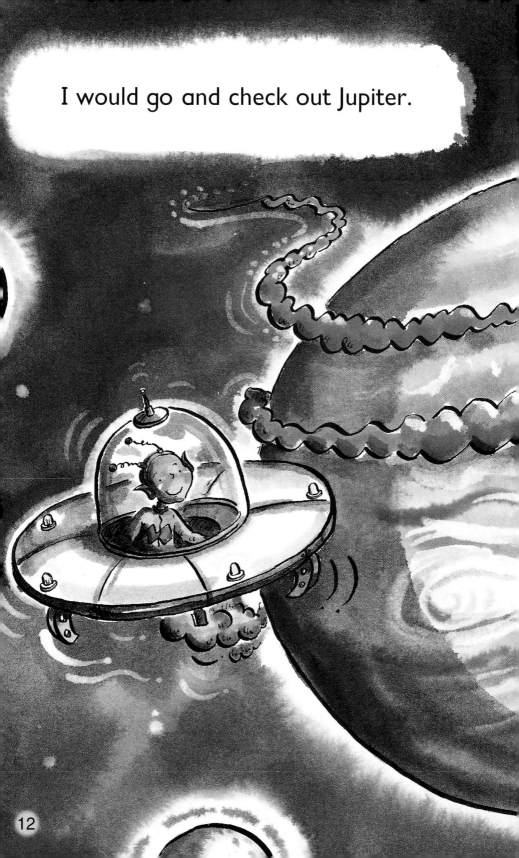

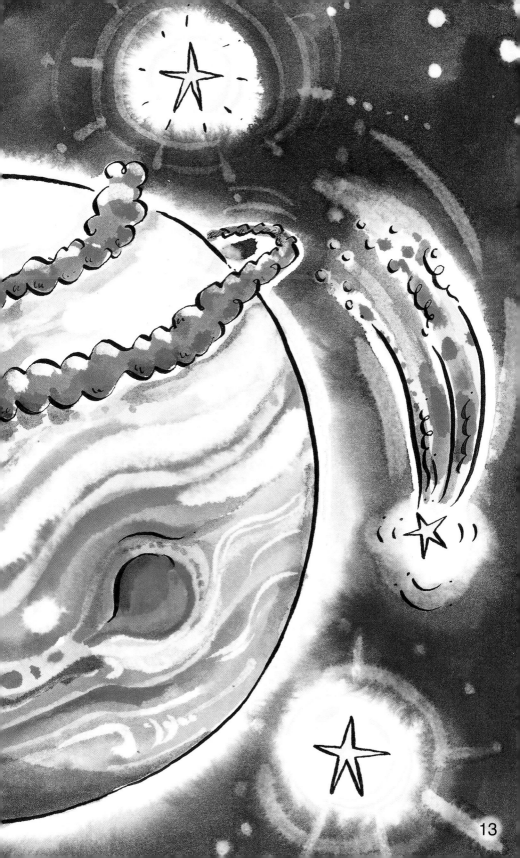

I would not have to brush
my hair.
I would fly a spaceship
to school.

I wish I were an alien.
An alien's life is cool!

17

I wish I were a boy on earth.
I would not live in space.
I would not have eleven arms.
And I would have a face.

The planets here are all the same.
And so are all the stars.

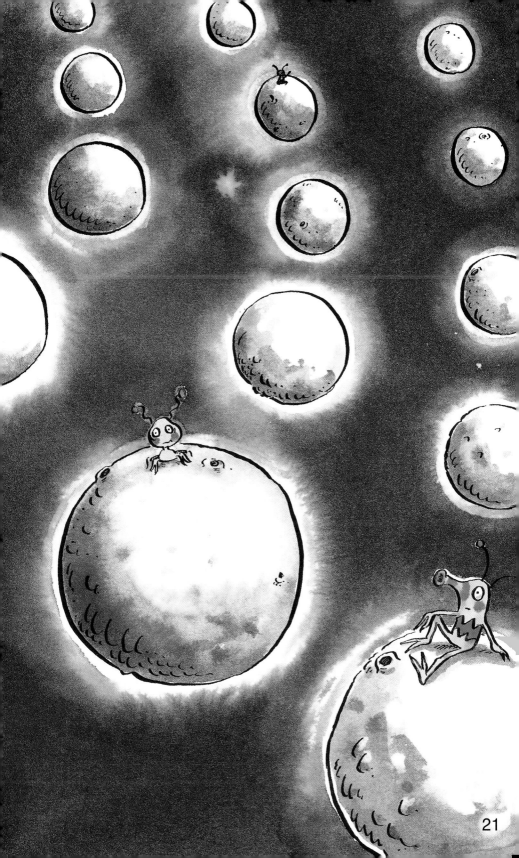

I want to ride on buses.

I want to drive in cars.

I want to play with children.

I want to go to school.

I wish I were a boy on earth.
An earth boy's life is cool!

Words I Know

around	want
live	were
play	wish
ride	would

Think About It!

1. Describe what a boy on earth looks like.
2. Describe what an alien might look like.
3. What kind of things does an alien do?
4. What kind of things does a boy on earth do?
5. This story is set in a rhyme. Read the story again. Point to the words that make the same sounds.

The Story and You

1. Do you ever wish you were someone else? Who?
2. Which would you rather be—an alien or a boy on earth?